Cellaring

a Novella

David Q. Hall

Printed in the United States of America
First Printing 2020
All rights reserved.

ISBN 13: 978-1-948894-12-8

Copyright © 2020 by David Q. Hall

Illustration by Maxine Hall

Tree Shadow Press

www.treeshadowpress.com

DEDICATION

In Memory of Ethel

ACKNOWLEDGMENTS

Credit and Gratitude is owed to my wife, the Rev. Maxine E. Hall, and my family for pushing me to spend "sheltering at home" time during the 2020 Covid-19 pandemic writing this novella.

"It'll be good therapy for you, Dad."

I believe it was.

CHAPTER ONE

It was dusk by the time that Alice and Vic turned on to the winding township road that would take them to the old family farmhouse. They had enjoyed a fun break by driving to the cheese factory in Shullsburg, where they stocked up on favorites - crumbly ten-year-old cheddar, cheese curds, triple-cream brie with wild mushrooms, and pepper jack.

The big, black SUV with darkly-tinted windows that had been behind them for several miles made the same turn and continued to follow them. It maintained the same separation, about one hundred yards back.

Alice resisted the urge to speed up her little plug-in hybrid sedan but glanced up and saw the SUV's head lights in her rearview mirror.

"He's still behind us."

Vic said, "Yes." They both reached the same conclusion. Their tail was not coincidental, and it was ominous.

They passed the ruins of an abandoned farmhouse that was the last place before reaching the old family homestead.

They were only a quarter of a mile from the gravel drive up to their destination. Alice was anxiously keeping an eye on the SUV when she saw it start to speed up and draw closer to their back bumper. Concerned that it might deliberately strike them from behind and spin them into the cattail-filled ditch along the township road, she pressed down hard on her accelerator. She practically did her own spin-out into the ditch as she fish-tailed around the turn into the lane up to the farmhouse.

Vic clutched the handle above the passenger door as he rocked violently from side-to-side with the sharp maneuver. He frantically tried to press 911 on his smartphone. No signal.

"I can't get a call placed," he said in frustration as they bounced at way too high of a speed up the gravel lane.

"Spotty reception out here," Alice said, gritting her teeth at an especially hard bump. "Or else they're jamming us."

Suddenly a nine-millimeter bullet shattered their back window and thudded into the back of her driver's seat. Somehow Alice managed to keep her hands on the steering wheel and the car on the lane as they both ducked their heads in panic.

"Holy shit!" Vic hollered. "What the..."

Another bullet from the SUV blew the left rear tire. Alice reflexively yanked the wheel to the right and skidded to a stop a few yards in front of the steps up to the porch of the house. The SUV sprayed gravel as it thundered to a stop a stone's throw behind them.

"Hurry, Vic," she shouted as she grabbed her laptop off the floor beneath her feet, scrambled out the driver's side and sprinted up to the front door. He was right behind her.

Three darkly-clad men with black knit hoods pulled over their heads and faces piled out of the SUV, each of them clutching AR-15 assault rifles. One of them fired a three-round burst as Alice and Vic threw open the door, routinely left unlocked in that low-crime, casual area. All three of the bullets struck Vic center-mass in his back, killing him instantly. His lifeless body slammed against the door as it toppled, literally pushing Alice inside as she rushed into the front entranceway and shoved the door shut behind her.

"Victor!" she screamed. But she had the presence of mind to lock and dead bolt the door as she convulsed with shock and grief. Alice looked wide-eyed in horror through the beveled glass of the door as the hooded assailants stomped up onto the porch, brandishing their automatic weapons. Two of them grabbed Vic's dead body under their arms, dragged the corpse to the back of the SUV, threw it onto a blue tarp, and slammed the back door shut. They quickly rejoined the third man, obviously the leader of the squad, and turned their attention to breaking into the house to get Alice.

Alice's terrified mind raced. *They'll be in here in a flash. Run out the back door? No, at least one of them will be back there already.* Her head swiveled frantically while her feet shuffled as though not knowing in what direction to step. *I can't escape out of this house. I have to hide, but...but, they'll search until they find me. Not the basement, not under the bed, no closet will work...of course, it's the only place.*

She lunged up the stairs to the second-floor safe room.

CHAPTER TWO

Exactly three days before...

Alice Louis welcomed her colleague and secret lover into her private office and closed the door. Victor Chernowski taught modern literature as an Assistant Professor at the University of Iowa, Iowa City, while Alice taught in the same capacity in the Creative Writing section of the English Department. Although neither was a professional journalist, both of them also contributed feature articles from time to time in the *Iowa City Daily Journal*. Alice especially admired investigative reporters and wondered at times if that was her true calling instead of teaching fiction writing to wannabe student authors. It was the end of the workday, and both had completed their classes and appointments that Wednesday.

"Wanna hit Micky's Irish Pub or Donnelly's for drink and supper?" Alice asked as Vic sat down at one of the chairs in front of her desk.

"Both of those places are really close to the Student Union and the hospital crowd," Vic said. "Lots of students and faculty. Why don't we go a little farther to the Big Grove Brewery?"

"Okay by me," Alice said.

"But first," Vic grew more serious in look and tone, "how goes it with 'The Project'?'"

Alice lowered her voice even more and at least matched his serious demeanor, "I think I'm getting really close to pulling it all together. I spoke *very* confidentially to John, the editor-in-chief of the *Daily Journal,* early this morning about wrapping it up and presenting it to him to go public, and almost to my surprise, it seems as though he would go with it. It would be the 'scoop' of all scoops, of course, and bring a lot of attention to the *Daily Journal.* Vault them to *Washington Post* or *New York Times* level of journalism. It's unbelievably exciting...and terribly scary, all mixed up together."

"Well, I think it's great," Vic smiled proudly, "and it really needs to be done. It would be an ultimate expression of 'speaking truth to power,' and should be as big a game changer as *The Pentagon Papers* or the Watergate investigation. What do you need to do yet to turn it over to John?"

"Well, I was thinking," Alice said, "why don't you and I leave as early as we can get away from here on Friday afternoon and drive over to my family's old homestead and farmhouse out in the country? You can help me with my notes and rough drafts, and I think I can get it all condensed and organized Friday evening, Saturday morning and evening, and go over it all a final time on Sunday before we drive back here to Iowa City. We'll take a well-earned break on Saturday and drive to Shullsburg for a fun lunch and cheese shopping at the great cheese factory there, then back to the farmhouse for Saturday evening...plus some fun of a different kind."

"Sounds like you have it well thought out and meticulously planned, as always. I'm in. But for now, meet you down at Big Grove? Say, 6:00?"

"It's a date," she smiled with great pleasure and an alluring wink. And Vic let himself out to pack up at his own office.

Alice had all of her notes, drafts, scanned evidence papers, witness affidavits, even some pertinent photos, on her highly encrypted laptop. She had taken the further precaution of copying everything on two encrypted thumb drives. She kept her laptop with her at all times, not even going to the restroom without it. The thumb drives she also had on her - one hidden in a cleverly disguised compartment in the thick heel of the running shoes she always wore. As soon as she could get out to the farmhouse this coming weekend, she would take the other copy and hide it in a secure, unfindable location in the stately old house. *Nothing anyone would think of. No "classic" hiding spot like a loose brick in the fireplace, or a wall safe behind a portrait of my great-grandfather, or a floor compartment under the old Persian rug in the parlor. And certainly not in an ice cube tray in the refrigerator freezer, or the big crock pot with flour in the kitchen,* she chuckled to herself. *No, I know just the perfect place where not a single soul would ever look. If my laptop is ever stolen or seized, or I run right out of my favorite shoes,* she chuckled again, *my second backup copy will be inside the old rooster weathervane up on the roof. Ready to sound the wakeup call for Justice to come forth.*

Alice looked at the clock on her smartphone. *Hour and a half until I have to drive down to Big Grove and meet Victor.* She leaned back in her ergonomic desk chair, closed her eyes, and thought about what she had put together. How she had obtained the incriminating material, and the effect she so dearly, desperately, hoped it would have on her city, her state, even the federal government. She hoped that it would be like that balancing game, *the one where you remove the wrong block in the bottom row and it brings the whole towering structure down. What's it called? Jergo? Jumble? Whatever.*

What Alice had compiled, almost by utter mistake at first, was concrete evidence that from little three-man township boards of supervisors, to city councils, to state legislative offices, to judgeships, to Congress and the federal administration itself...key, powerful offices and positions were literally bought and paid for. Huge sums not only being spent on things like political campaigns, but huge sums being paid for regular appointments. Key resignations were bought so that paid-for appointments could be made to fill them temporarily. *The oft-made contention that we have the worst system of government that money can buy? Well, I have proof of the corruption and the rot of greed and money. Dante's Inferno couldn't compare to the level of evil and sin I can document.*

She had realized as bit-by-bit the pieces had come together that her material was not only explosive, it was dangerous to the absolute extreme, including to her personally. Which was why she had been as cautious and secretive as a human could be. Vic had been let in on her secret because she trusted him completely, even with her very life. A few of her best sources, her deep confidants, knew that she was putting something together, but she had been ultra-careful not to let anyone else know of the breadth and depth of her project. Even John the editor-in-chief had only a partial picture of what he assumed would be a limited exposé.

It was almost time to turn off the lights, shut the door, and head out for drinks and supper. The first thumb drive was in the hidden shoe compartment. The second was in an invisible pocket in the lining of her laptop case. Alice slipped on her jacket against the early evening chill, tucked the laptop into its case, fastened a tough chain that latched her case onto a stout silver bracelet around her left wrist like a diplomatic courier with classified papers, and opened her office door to leave. But first she paused to think, *Here goes. I sure hope this works, and that I'll be back in this office and the classrooms next Monday...after meeting early with John.*

It's been said that Life is what happens to you while you're on your way to somewhere else. Similar sentiments have been attributed to John Lennon and to Allen Saunders before him. Alice had no way of knowing where she was being taken in her life from that point.

CHAPTER THREE
Exactly three days later...

As Alice reached the second floor, clutching her laptop case literally for dear life, she heard the antique beveled glass of the front door being shattered. A black-gloved hand reached through the broken glass and bent leading and groped for the dead bolt and door handle lock.

No time to be paralyzed and gawk, she thought. *I have to get to the safe room.*

She dashed down the upstairs hall and into the big master bedroom. She closed the door behind her as quietly as she could and crept over to the large antique, double-doored wardrobe against the side wall on the opposite side of the room.

Many years ago, her grandfather, a farmer, carpenter and all-around handyman, had constructed the safe room. No one had ever envisioned anything like Alice's current emergency. Rather, in that prairie country with annual tornado season, it had been intended for a family tornado shelter. Grandpa had converted a small storage room adjacent to the master bedroom with only one door from the bedroom into the safe room. He had reinforced the framing all around the old storage space with heavy, six-by-six wooden beams. Additional inch-thick planks had given the walls, floor, and ceiling more-than-double thickness.

The original hollow-core door had been replaced with a solid steel door with interior slide locks near the top and bottom of the door, and a chain lock in the middle. The intent was that in the event of a crushing of the outer bedroom due to cave-in of the roof of the house, the door could not be crushed open. And because he was a master carpenter with a perfectionist streak, the outside of the door was covered with rustic planking that perfectly matched the interior of the old wardrobe. When shut, it fit and blended so snugly that it was indistinguishable from the rest of the inside of the wardrobe. You wouldn't even know there was a door there. And instead of a handle by which to open it and gain access to the safe room, all one had to do was push against an ornamental, carved medallion in the middle of the back of the wardrobe, and the heavy door would swing smoothly open...so long as no one was inside and had locked it shut.

Alice and her younger sister, Jane, had sometimes played by entering the safe room, although they were very strictly forbidden from ever trying to lock themselves in. Alice gleefully referred to herself as "the witch in the wardrobe" when she snuck into the safe room.

The safe room had been wired to a new intercom system that Alice's father had installed several years ago, so that anyone inside the room could communicate with people in other rooms in the spacious, old farmhouse. It also had cell phone and internet access, as well as a radio system. The room was stocked with bottled water and non-perishable food items to be able to support a family of as many as six people for up to a week. The two folding cots were supplemented with rolled up sleeping bags. There was even a small bookcase with a number of classic works of fiction, as well as some favorite family games. And very important - a first aid kit, flashlights, rain gear, and a strong rope.

Since the room had never been envisioned as a defense against unheard-of home invasion, there was no security system panel or viewing monitor. It was also unusual for a tornado shelter space to be located on the second floor instead of on a ground floor or basement level, but Grandpa had decided that the old storage room was the most usable space in the house, and that his reinforcements of the structure would leave it intact even if the rest of the house collapsed.

There were no windows, but he had planned for emergency exit in the event that the house did collapse around the room. There was a trap door - also bolted from the inside - placed in the ceiling of the safe room. It opened into the spacious attic of the old house through the attic floor. There was no access to the safe room from the attic unless someone inside the room unbolted the trap door.

But even though her frantic impulse was to rush into the safe room as quickly as possible, Alice had enough presence of mind to realize that with one assailant posted outside and two searching the house for her, it would take at least a couple of minutes for them to clear the first floor and its possible hiding spots. Even a bit longer if at least one of them went down into the basement before they headed upstairs. She decided to try a desperate diversion.

She tied together the two sheets on the master bedroom bed as fast as she could, pushed up a back window, tied one end of the joined sheets to the old radiator under the window, and tossed the loose end out and down the side of the house. To further try to sell her diversion, she grabbed a small statue off of a bedside table and tossed it into the dark woods near the side of the house. As she had hoped, the statue made a rustling noise as it struck the underbrush down below. *I hope that was loud enough to get the outside guy's attention.* She didn't linger at the window to see if it had. But it had.

Alice scooped up her laptop case off of the dresser, patted her jacket pocket to make sure that her cell phone was still there and hadn't fallen out during all of the exertion, and went very quickly over to the wardrobe on the adjacent wall. She swung open the wardrobe's twin doors, reached in and pushed against the ornamental medallion, and sure enough...the safe room door swung open on its interior hinges. She reached back, pulled the wardrobe doors shut again, stepped partway into the safe room, and then turned back and pushed together the clothes, robes, table runners and loose hangers on the rod at the top of the interior of the wardrobe. She entered the safe room, turned on the single battery-powered lamp, and swung the safe room door closed again. It fit snugly and imperceptibly into the back wall of the wardrobe, and she secured all of the locks on the inside. *Time will tell,* she clenched her jaw, *but maybe I'm safe for a little bit.* She sat down on a folding chair inside to calm herself with deep breathing and think as best she could.

What now?

CHAPTER FOUR

The hit squad had planned meticulously for this eventuality. If they didn't eliminate the targets before they were able to reach and enter the house, if one or both accessed the interior, then they would proceed according to protocol. One of the squad members would post outside, especially watching the back that led to pasture, and the side near the adjoining woods. The other two would conduct a by-the-manual sweep of the levels of the house.

First priority was to acquire the laptop and any copies of files stored on thumb or other drives. Second and simultaneous was to eliminate the subjects. There was no need to interrogate or take prisoner. They were to leave no physical evidence behind. No brass casings, no prints, no DNA samples. And no bodies to autopsy. The black ops garments and footgear they wore would be destroyed without a trace as soon as they returned to base, as well as even the deep-lugged tires on their SUV. No one would ever have anything to use as evidence for any future inquiry.

Their equipment was state-of-the-art, and included night vision goggles, thermal binoculars, closed circuit mounted phones, and a variety of lethal weaponry besides the AR-15 assault rifles and the 9mm Glocks. They even carried SOG F01T tactical Tomahawks and Ka-Bar Becker BK9 combat Bowie knives. Whatever might do the job best, they had it.

The squad leader and his number two had just about completed clearing the downstairs and basement levels when Number Three heard the "crunch" noise in the side woods. He immediately radioed the other two. "Got some noise in the woods along the house. Will check it out. Over."

"Copy that," replied the leader. "I'll send Number Two to assist."

"Squad leader," Number Three came back, "I'm looking at a bedsheet rope dangling from a second story window on this woods side. She may be trying to escape through the trees. Over."

"Copy, Number Three. Number Two Is on his way, double quick. Over and out."

The transmission had barely ended when number two joined up with Number Three, and the two of them started into the woods, searching for tracks, disturbed foliage, broken branches, movement up ahead, any sign that someone had gone that way.

The squad leader stayed on the main floor of the house, near the elaborate, carved wooden staircase leading up to the second floor. A successful operation depended on being prepared for any eventualities, and he didn't want to leave a primary exit unwatched in case the woman hadn't really tried to escape into the woods. In either case, he knew they'd soon have her, and more important, the computer and drives. He didn't know what information was contained on those drives, but he didn't need to know. It was sufficient for the squad to know that people at the very top had made its acquisition a matter of highest priority.

Several minutes had passed when Number Two came back on the line.

"Squad Leader, do you copy?"

"Go ahead, Number Two. Over."

"There's absolutely no sign that she went this way. All we could find was some broken ceramic. May have tossed it out that window as a diversion. Over."

"Copy that. You two get back here on the double. We're heading upstairs. Over and out."

CHAPTER FIVE

Alice had no illusions that her phony escape out the window would fool her pursuers for very long. *I wish it would, but these guys are pros. Maybe military special ops. Or former military. Maybe private contractors.*

Partly to calm herself and give her something to think about other than being immobilized with terror, she wondered who might have sent them after a couple of university assistant professors.

I mean, talk about overkill. She shuddered at her mental choice of that word. She wasn't ready for the real possibility of being killed. Which forced her to think for a horrifying instant about Victor. But she shoved that thought and feeling down as deep as she could. Her survival depended on maintaining complete focus on her own plight.

She went back for a moment to wondering about who was behind this attack. *Could it be military? Had one of her few confidants or sources leaked that she had evidence of military money being diverted to buy politicians and their votes? Could it be big, wealthy corporations? The industrial/military complex Eisenhower had warned about years ago? Had the targeting been assigned by politicians themselves?* It was all fruitless speculation and fretting on her part, she realized. The only thinking that mattered at this point was how to find a way out of her self-imposed imprisonment. Much like her knotted sheets dangling out the window, Alice's hiding spot was simply a little more elaborate diversion. *This safe room will not be safe forever. But maybe it will keep me safe long enough to think of something else. But one thing I know. The information I have has to get out for everyone to know. The truth needs to survive, even if I don't.*

She took a deep breath and reached in her pocket for her cell phone. But despite the cell phone and internet capability of the safe room, there was still no signal. *I must have been right back on the road. They have to be using a jammer.* There was no old-fashioned land line phone in the relatively new safe room. *But at least I have electricity.* She thought it would be prudent at least to charge her cell phone in case it became usable. *Or not,* she grimaced. *No charging. They must have cut the power.*

Alice was right. The hit squad had no need for electric lights with their night vision and thermal imaging capability. The three black ops men had now climbed the stairs and were going room to room to find her. With all of the thickness of walls, floor and ceiling, as well as the perfectly camouflaged steel door in the back of the wardrobe, she couldn't really hear their stealthy movements, but she had no trouble forming a mental picture of their sweep of the second floor rooms.

And two of them - the squad leader and the number three - eased into the master bedroom, checked under the bed, cleared the private bath attached, and looked behind furniture. Squad leader made brief check of the sheets hanging out of the raised window, looked outside to each side and up, and concluded that there was no way the woman could head anywhere but down if she would have climbed out of the window.

They saved the antique wardrobe for last, as the most logical hiding place. Squad leader held his automatic rifle at the ready as number three crouched down and flipped open one of the doors of the wardrobe. Nothing but hanging clothes and other items. He crouched even further and crept over to flip open the other door. They had no particular reason to suspect that their target might be armed, but they prepared for every possible contingency. A careless operative was apt to become a dead operative. Still no one in there.

Number Three rose up and grabbed armfuls of the hanging clothes, throwing them out on the bedroom floor. Exposing the inner back of the wardrobe revealed that there was no hidden door to anywhere else.

"She's not anywhere in this room or any of the others upstairs here," squad leader reported to number two as the three huddled out in the hallway. "That leaves only the attic, and somewhere there needs to be an access to the attic. Number two, you stay here and keep eyes and ears just in case, we'll find that attic access and check it out.

They discovered the drop-down hatch and pull-down ladder in a hall closet that they had checked a bit before. It was when they cautiously climbed into the attic and began to move around up there that Alice finally heard some scraping noise above her in the safe room as the two hit men shoved boxes and stored items around, looking for where she might be hiding. But their attic search was also futile, and the two climbed back down to the second floor.

"Not up there either," the squad leader grumbled with a mixture of agitation, disgust and just the smallest bit of what was almost respect. He wasn't ready to admit that they had been outmaneuvered by a mere teacher, but eliminating this particular target was a tad bit more difficult than any of them could have expected.

"Men, she has to be in here somewhere. We saw her go through the front door. You two determined that she hadn't escaped out the upstairs window and into the woods or anywhere outside. And there's no way that she would have the skills to move out there and leave no tracks or sign of any kind.

"There has to be a hiding place so expertly disguised that our standard clearing protocols didn't detect it. Nothing under the staircase?"

"Nope," said Number Two. "And nobody anywhere in the basement."

"Well, then, we go over it all again. And make sure you use the thermal imaging. There has to be a body heat signature somewhere."

CHAPTER SIX

An elaborate office overlooking the Mall
in Washington, D.C.
Earlier that same day...

A deputy secretary of an agency in the federal administration named Chris, a high-ranking officer named Robert, with an office in the Pentagon, and the CEO of a major defense contractor met in Chris's office Saturday morning, coincidentally about the same time that Alice and Victor were wrapping up to take their break and go on their side trip to the cheese factory in Shullsburg. As the host, Chris poured brandy-laced coffee for all three of them and began their discussion.

"Anything to report on our joint project?" he asked his two guests.

"A three-man squad is near the border of Iowa and Wisconsin as we speak," said the officer. "They eliminate the problem there and secure the package, no problem."

"With total discretion and without a trace?"

"Affirmative. And they're not active duty and entirely off the books."

The CEO spoke next. "And last night that reckless editor at the *Iowa Daily Journal* suffered a catastrophic traffic accident on his commute home to Coralville. It wasn't fatal, yet, but he's in a coma in ICU and prognosis is, shall I say, doubtful."

"And the key sources, collaborators, leakers, potential witnesses we know about?" Chris continued.

"Well," the Pentagon officer replied a little hesitantly, "we're in the process of evaluating those now, but it will help tremendously to have those drives. That way we can more thoroughly identify who might present a threat...to our, ah, 'arrangement.'"

The CEO added, "We did learn, however, of two sub-contractors who were a little too careless in supplying information about, shall we say, 'incentives,' when she interviewed them. They both claim that they thought they were speaking harmlessly and 'off the record.' After all, it was all business as usual in their experience. One of them has been transferred to a division in Alaska, the other received 'corrective' measures and is repenting while he recuperates. They and any others will be monitored and quieted if necessary."

Chris sipped his coffee and smiled in a manner that even the other two thought seemed sinister. "Good. Just a minor blip, gentlemen, all successful ventures experience an occasional bump in the road of success." He sipped again with satisfaction.

The CEO was very capable of proceeding ruthlessly in his business dealings, but he frankly felt a twinge of discomfort about going so far as hit squads and arranging fatal "accidents." He was extremely hesitant about expressing that disquiet, but finally almost blurted, "But couldn't we just deny, discredit, obfuscate, bury her shaky claims in our usual blizzard of disinformation and posturing?"

Chris leaned forward ominously in his expensive Italian leather chair, "You're a businessman, Jack. You of all guys should appreciate cost effectiveness and PR. Why even allow a wisp of smoke? It makes more people suspect that there's really a fire behind it all. No, this is for the best. Think of it as a virus threatening the health of our body of fine work. The sooner we eradicate it, the better for all. Everybody's profiting from this apple cart. Don't upset it." He leaned back again and sipped some more. Chris liked both fine, limited reserve coffee and expensive brandy...whatever the time of day.

One of the CEO's many divisions dealt in a variety of commodities, and Chris enjoyed making "folksy" analogies to his business affairs. And despite the casualness of his metaphors, Chris was well aware that illegal burning of indigenous rainforest lands in the Amazon, virus infections among the third world workers on the plantations, and even the importing of apples from the world's largest producer in China, were all constant challenges the CEO had to handle. Message received.

The three adjourned their highly secretive meeting in agreement. Nothing to see here.

CHAPTER SEVEN

Back in the safe room...

Alice looked at her watch. A full hour had passed since Victor and she had been chased up to the farmhouse. She continued to repress her mental images and horror at his death and tried to focus on her predicament. And while her survival was paramount, she really, truly, believed that revealing the truth of her discoveries was even more important. And she had to find some way of accomplishing that objective.

By now they have to have figured out that I did not actually leave this house and escape into the woods. One way or another they're eventually going to find this safe room. God, I wish we had put that security monitor in here. Maybe I could have had some inkling of where they are and what they're doing.

Well, it's completely dark outside now. And would be in here if it weren't for this little battery-powered lamp. And how old is that battery? It won't provide a charge for very much longer. I have to get out of this temporary hiding place and the only way of doing that is up through the hatch and into the attic. And hope against all hope that they don't go back up there to search some more when I do it.

But if - BIG If - I can get up there while they're still re-searching the lower parts of the house...then what? I can even use an attic vent to struggle up to the roof, but again, then what? If I made it down to the ground without breaking my damn neck, they'd track me down without a doubt. The house to the east is that abandoned, falling-down place, and it's the proverbial country mile to the Anderson's to the west.

But in the sometimes trite category of "desperate times call for desperate measures," the only choice finally dawned upon Alice.

The old root cellar!

CHAPTER EIGHT

*G*enerations before Alice, her grandfather's grandfather had homesteaded on this prairie land. The first rough dwelling was a very primitive but inexpensive sod house. Lacking a drilled well for water, it was located about a hundred yards north of the later house, near to a small prairie pothole or pond for water supply. It had been constructed by cutting the tough prairie sod into long strips or blocks and laying it like natural bricks to make walls. It was a crude dwelling, but provided the necessary shelter against blizzards and cold, thunderstorms, and even the sweltering summer sun. Meanwhile, surrounding prairie sod was laboriously dug into and plowed to be able to plant their first crops.

The sod house was replaced a few years later as materials were procured to be able to build a more satisfactory wooden frame house, modest and one-story at first. The original frame house was eventually replaced by Alice's great-grandfather with the much grander farmhouse in which she now hid. The old sod house was long-gone, crumbling into ruin, and then the land smoothed over and also planted. But the original root cellar was still there.

Close to the little pond, which was maintained by a small natural spring and seepage, on its south shore, was a low hillock or mound. And into the small knoll, facing the site of the original sod house, Alice's great-great grandfather and his boys had dug an old-fashioned root cellar in order to store produce, milk, wine, cider, beer, even meat, pretty much anything perishable in that era before refrigeration. Many vegetable and other items could be kept for months and months.

The root cellar was another ingenious, crude, but highly effective, feature of pioneer homesteading and old, traditional farms. Alice's ancestors had constructed theirs to be as efficient and permanent as possible. It had an outer, short, heavy plank door, a passageway of a few yards that had to be negotiated by hunching over, but which had been sturdily reinforced with rough timbers to prevent cave-ins. Then there was an inner door of same design and materials. Entry through the inner door took one into the main chamber, which was roughly square and lined with more heavy planks as walls and shelving. A reinforced ceiling was made the same way, with a couple of interior support posts, again guarding against sagging and possible cave-in. The floor was hardened dirt.

The design and construction kept precious and perishable food supplies at controlled temperatures and steady humidity. Food was kept just above freezing during the often brutal winters, and quite cool during the summer heat. The short entranceway or "corridor" - some called it a "porch" - helped greatly to keep frost out. From childhood Alice and her ancestors had been taught to shut the first, outer door before they opened the second, inner one.

Even in Alice's time the root cellar had continued to be used, and in later years she delighted in thinking of it as a kind of "hobbit house." Even more important to her than its storage capabilities, when Alice and her sister Jane visited the farm, they loved to go down to the root cellar to play, to imagine, to get away from the boring adults, to entertain friends, and to keep cool before window air conditioners were finally introduced to the old house. They called it "cellaring," accompanied by smiles and giggles.

One other feature about storage in the old root cellar was that it was a perfectly fine place to keep long-term supplies of canned goods, preserves, jellies, jam, even holiday fruit cakes made months before Thanksgiving, Christmas and New Year. As primitive as the place was, it kept things at better temperature, humidity, and cleaner than the dirty, old farmhouse basement. And frankly, less vulnerable to rodents and what the sisters called "creepy-crawlies."

Sometimes when young Alice was spending time with her grandmother at the farm, Grandma would be "baking up a storm," and she would send Alice down to the root cellar for a variety of preserved fruits.

"I be 'glazin'" Grandma would tell her, "so get me a jar of peaches, apricots, and, oh, some dried prunes, too."

It was an errand of joy for Alice, for not only was "cellaring" just lots of fun, the results of Grandma's efforts were incomparably delicious!

Over the long years since its construction and active use, the hillock and the root cellar had become overgrown with tall grasses and brush. The land wasn't actively farmed anymore, the once-productive fields being converted to just pasture and a few crops like hay or a little buckwheat. There was a small, overgrown garden next to the farmhouse, opposite the woods side. In fact, the outer door of the root cellar had been overgrown and hidden from anything but close scrutiny from a few feet away. You had to push and force your way in order to open the door, but the marvelous handmade hinges still allowed the door to be pushed in and open. It was an almost perfect hiding place.

CHAPTER NINE

$\mathbf{A}$s Alice wrestled with what to do, where she could go, the lethal hit squad had once again cleared the basement and the downstairs rooms. This time, to be doubly sure she couldn't be hiding in any secret space, they employed a thermal imaging camera that was designed for weapons targeting and extreme border surveillance. It weighed more than fifty pounds, but they carried it in the back of the Black SUV just in case it was needed in unusual circumstances. It penetrated and saw much farther than the usual thermal binoculars.

Satisfied that she wasn't tucked behind some hidden panel or in some secret compartment, Number Two and Number Three Lugged the camera up the stairs and went room by room as before. And as before, of some small help to Alice, they saved the master bedroom for last.

They only had to worry about under the floor and behind the interior walls, there not being enough room in the two exterior walls for a human body to fit.

"There," said Number Two intently, "there's a small, hidden room behind this old wardrobe. And a faint body heat signature, as though someone is in there, or recently was."

In addition to their usual weaponry, the squad had also snatched an old-fashioned log-splitting maul with a five-pound steel head from the basement tools. Number Three grabbed the maul and started swinging fiercely at the back wooden panels of the wardrobe. Quickly he began clanging the splitting edge of the maul against the steel core of the disguised door to the safe room.

"Solid steel core to that hidden door," said the leader. "That's where she is. And her computer and drives. No use battering our way through that door to get in there. Number Two, let's blow it open with some C4."

Number Two fished a brick of the Composition C-4 out of a compartment in his backpack and taped it to the steel door, making sure that the explosion would blow in the right direction. He inserted a blasting cap or PETN-based detonating cord into the block of malleable explosive. The other two stepped back out of the bedroom as he initiated the detonation. C4 has high cutting ability and was favored for just this kind of use.

Alice could hear the bangs of the maul as it split apart the back of the wardrobe and clanged against the steel-core door. Barely a minute before she had judged that the assailants had to have reached the second floor, and she had dropped open the escape hatch into the attic, hoping and praying that none of them had gone on up into the attic. As she made her way as fast as she could crouch over to the north attic vent, she uncoiled the length of rope that had been stored in the safe room. She easily removed the vent panel and lowered one end of the rope after tying the other end to an attic crossbeam.

She tossed her padded laptop case down to the grassy lawn. Then she wriggled through the old vent hole, which was just wide and tall enough for her slim, five-foot three frame to fit through. But before she slid down the rope to the ground, she made a hasty decision to complete a plan she had made earlier. She braced her right sneaker against the edge of the vent opening and swung her left foot up to catch the roof edge. She grabbed the roof edge with her left hand, while keeping the rope draped around her right elbow. Pushing off with her right leg, and pulling up with both hands and her extended left leg, she managed to leverage herself over the roof edge and onto the roof.

It was a rash, if not crazy, effort, but once up on the roof, she scurried over to the weather vane at the ridge top, tilted the brass rooster to one side, and stuck the second thumb drive with all of her stored information, documentations, photos, witness statements, every bit of evidence she had gathered over all those months, under the brass base. Then she clamped it back in place.

She had no trouble hearing the explosion as she completed her slide down to the ground, climbing rope-style. *I damn well hope they enjoyed that one,* she grimaced as she shook herself for a second, grabbed up her laptop case, and sprinted across the lawn and into the back pasture.

Alice had no idea if it might work, but just before she climbed up out of the safe room and into the attic, she had taken a large, glass bottle of lamp oil that had been stored in the room among the emergency supplies. It had been intended, of course, to use in two, old-fashioned, oil-burning hurricane lamps in the case of power failure in a severe storm or tornado. She had taken the lamp oil and duct-taped it heavily onto the inside middle of the steel-core door.

She had no idea that the hit squad would eventually blow the door open with explosive, but she thought if they tried to batter the door down, they might break the lamp oil bottle. Then possibly, the oil would splatter and drain down the length of the door, and maybe, just maybe, a spark from striking against the steel door would ignite the oil and at least slow down the bastards' entry into the safe room. She figured it was a really long-shot try, but it was the only "booby trap" she could think of before she escaped up into the attic.

The C4 explosion had exactly that effect, however. It not only blew open and severely bent in the door, but it also ignited the lamp oil, much to the real surprise of the assailants. Before long, and before they could gain their entry, virtually the entire room was engulfed in flames.

"Well, men," said the squad leader, "it looks like we won't have to waste any more rounds on target elimination. We'll just have to put out the flames and retrieve the body and the package. Number Three, go down to the kitchen and bring back that fire extinguisher."

It took a good twenty minutes before they had the fire extinguished and could actually enter the charred safe room. And when they did and shoved aside the blackened debris, real frustration and bewilderment set in for perhaps the first time in many well-executed missions. Their target and the package were nowhere to be found.

"Goddammit to hell," the leader barked. "Where'd she go?"

CHAPTER TEN

B y this time, it was past ten o'clock Central Standard Time, and the plan requirement was for the squad leader to report to his superior in special ops by encrypted sat phone by 11:30 p.m. Eastern. And the report was to be "mission accomplished" so that his superior could in turn make a positive report to the Pentagon officer before midnight. How hard could it be to eliminate and procure when the target was a couple of college profs? It wasn't like top Taliban insurgents in Afghanistan, or a Hezbollah chief in the Middle East.

"She has to have made it out of here and outside somewhere, boss," Number Two said.

"Well, we better catch up to her in the next twenty minutes," the leader spit, "or my ass is in a wringer, and yours is going to be blistered. Downstairs and out, now!"

The three hit men ran down the hall and down the staircase and split up on the main floor. Number Two went out the front door to check on whether the woman had tried to go down the drive to the township road. Number Three was sent out the back door into the back yard, garden area and toward the back pasture. The squad leader checked all sides of the house, and quickly found the dangling rope hanging from the opened attic vent.

Well, he grumbled silently, *I guess that answers my question as to how she got out of the hidden room. Now which direction did she head?*

He radioed the other two to meet up with him as soon as he spotted a fresh track pointed in the direction of the back pasture. "She's headed into the back forty. Let's run her down. We should have her and the package in a matter of minutes."

He caught up to Number Three, and Number Two reached both of them soon after. *We can still get her by 2230.* If not, he really didn't look forward to making that sat call. *My next goddamned mission could end up being solo in Antarctica.*

Alice had succeeded in buying herself almost a half hour of time and space from her pursuers. Although she was still in heightened panic mode and on the verge of physical and mental exhaustion, she still maintained exceptional control and focus. She fully expected that they would have no great difficulty tracking her, with their state-of-the-art technology and highly trained experience. She had neither the learned skill nor the time to make her way without leaving any kind of "sign," but she had retained her unusual common sense.

Shit, for all I know they could even have a tracking dog in the back of that SUV. Fortunately, it didn't occur to her that in that possibility, however unlikely, it would be accompanied by Victor's corpse that the real beasts had tossed in there.

She couldn't afford the time to try to hide or obscure her

tracks across the pasture, but instead of heading directly toward the old root cellar, she veered off toward the other end of the small pond. The prairie pothole was in a low swale surrounded by low knolls or hillocks like the farmhouse side where the root cellar was located. All around the pond was a wide fringe of low-lying marshy wetland with cattails, rushes, brush and an occasional short willow.

She deliberately slogged her way through the east end of the marsh vegetation and into the shallow water of the pond. Before long, her tracks disappeared in the water and pond bottom. Those that remained continued to point to the north.

Alice waded quickly along parallel to the south shore of the pond - scattering a small flock of ducks roosting in the water - until she reached a point closest to the hillock where the old root cellar was located. She figured that she had used up close to twenty minutes of time since she fled the house. In yet another effort to avoid leaving sign of her true path, when she waded up to the marshy wetland closest to the cellar, she removed the flashlight and other items from her jacket pockets and clutched her jacket and precious laptop case as she approached a hard, sandy bottom patch with a small opening in the marsh cattails and rushes. It was where Jane, she, friends and family members could enter the pond and swim or splash around over the years.

She laid her jacket down on the water's edge, partly in the wet, and partly on the dry shore. She then stepped on the jacket, took a few short steps until she reached as far as she could go without leaving the jacket. Still clutching her laptop case with her left hand, she turned around, reached back, and pulled the jacket toward her without stepping off of it. She twisted the jacket so that the part she wasn't standing on could be brought in front of her and enable another three short steps in the direction of the cellar. She had also grabbed a dead branch she found in the marsh grass and reached back so that she could roughly brush away any marks left in the sand and dirt by scrunching her jacket and standing on it.

Alice was well aware that her efforts to avoid leaving tracks and marks on the ground where she went was crude and wouldn't hold up under close examination by an expert tracker, but she counted on several facts. First, it was night, and even with their night vision goggles the bastards were unlikely to pick up very faint brush marks. Second, they had a large area of acres and acres to try to find her sign, and unless they did have a scent dog, it would take a lot of time and effort to come across the very faint evidence that she had come this way. And third, the trail they did have to follow at least suggested that she had gone north, into the water. And either she made her way to the north shore, where they would search fruitlessly for a continuing trail, or she simply gave up and drowned. If they concluded the latter, they would have to engage in a whole 'nother search mode to try to find her body, and especially the damn laptop and drives.

Fortunately, the distance to the root cellar was short and only took about ten minutes for Alice to negotiate with her moving her jacket around to step onto. Also, the last few yards were covered with the wild brush that had grown up over the years, totally obscuring the outer door to the cellar. She gathered up her jacket with her laptop, carefully pushed her way through the brush without breaking any branches or displacing anything, and there it was. And a good thing, because as she had roughly but correctly guessed, her time margin had been used up, and the hit squad had reached the marsh and pond at its far east end.

CHAPTER ELEVEN

The woman was nowhere in sight. Her tracks had led the squad very plainly to the east end of this prairie pothole, but it was obvious that they led into the marshy wetland and toward the water. And the leader was out of time in his assigned schedule. He backed up several yards to the top of the hillock leading down to the pond and reluctantly made his required call.

"Operation Prairie Falcon reporting, over."

Command responded immediately, "Copy squad leader. What's your 1020 and do we have 1024? Over."

The squad leader knew that he was asking their precise location, and whether their assignment had been completed. "Our 1020 is on the farm still, and we have a 1080, over."

He didn't have any choice but to report that they had a chase in progress. He gritted his teeth and held his phone a little away from his ear at the comeback.

The commander dropped standard transmission codes and virtually exploded. "What the hell are you telling me?

How could one of my best black op squads mess up a simple mission like this one? Unless you fix this with a 1024 NOW, I'm 1076 tomorrow 900 hours! 10-3." And the transmission ended before the squad leader was tempted to reply 10-1, "unable to copy." He really didn't want to face the commander in person, but the 1076 was a promise to be en route to their location tomorrow morning by 9:00 a.m. unless they could complete the assignment that night.

Damn, this is fubar like I've never dealt with before. Somehow we have to run her down. There was nothing to do but keep searching.

On the other end, the commander had to suck it up and call his boss at the Pentagon. Despite the late hour, he had the superior officer's private, encrypted cell phone number. Even worse, he would have to wake him up to tell him extremely unwelcome news. He had his own feelings of "fubar," f...ed up beyond all recognition.

An emergency meeting was called and held at the same high-end office and hosted in the same way by agency deputy director, Chris, the Pentagon officer, Robert, and the nervous CEO of the defense contractor, at 7:00 a.m. the next morning. It was Sunday, and no one of the three was pleased at having to disturb their Sunday routines to conference like this.

Chris took a slug of his usual enhanced coffee and stared out the floor-to-ceiling window overlooking the Mall. Normally the view reinforced his feelings of status, privilege, power and how good it was to be one of the "elect" on both God's green Earth and in the corridors of federal government...and he didn't mean public elections.

Democracy be damned, he sometimes thought. *Control of everything is meant for people like me. It's our blessedness and right way of life that has to be protected. To hell with the rest of them. Life, liberty and the achievement of happiness is for us and ours.* But now the sacredness and quietude of his Sunday morning had been disrupted by this foul-up out on the Midwestern prairie. And his view was likewise befouled. *Dammit.*

His co-collaborators from the military and corporate world looked down at the expensive Persian rug, up at the valuable paintings, at each other nervously, and waited for him to say something. When Chris did speak, it was with slightly clenched teeth and in cold, controlled tones.

"Any word?"

The Pentagon officer cleared his throat and said, "Not yet," hastening to add, "but it should be soon."

"Soon," Chris betrayed both skepticism and discontent. "Your best has been after this mere woman, this civilian teacher, for what? Nigh onto twelve hours?" It was not really a question. "And what hard evidence do you have that this incredibly soft target will finally be eliminated *soon*?" The sarcasm was not at all subtle. "And most important, where is the package?"

That was a bit more of a question...and something of an anxious one.

The officer shifted slightly uncomfortably in his chair. "There's really no place she can safely hide, and no way to escape and disappear," he said. "Wherever she's holed up out there, they'll find her. But the search has been in the dark of night, and complicated by..." His voice trailed off and he wished he hadn't said that last sentence. He realized once the words left his mouth that it sounded like irrelevant, pathetic excuse-making. *Better I shut up.*

Chris didn't make any attempt to hide his disgust. Once again the CEO found himself wishing that he wasn't even there, or at least that he could disappear into the soft leather of the club chair. But also, once again, he just couldn't keep quiet.

"Gentlemen, gentlemen, something has to be done about this. Do you have any idea how much money I have riding on this arrangement of ours?"

Of course they did. Pretty much down to the exact dollar. The other two merely looked at him, and he decided that *he* should probably just shut up.

Chris looked back at the officer and spoke again. "You should tell us what steps are being taken to rectify this situation and accomplish the mission. And before the Secretary himself starts lopping off heads." *Including mine.*

"Unless I receive the 'all good' word within the next hour," the officer replied, "the commander of the off-the-books special op squads will board a plane and fly out there himself this morning, and he'll have all of the resources at his disposal to make sure the mission is accomplished with no further hitches."

Chris lowered his chin, took another sip - *This doesn't taste as soothing this morning, for some reason* - and humphed. "Could have believed that I was told that before." He looked up again. "Keep me posted every step of the way." He looked over to the CEO, "And we certainly don't want to toss any good money after bad, do we?" That question was rhetorical.

CHAPTER TWELVE
In the root cellar...eight hours before

Alice pushed open the root cellar door. Once in the "porch," she shoved the outer door shut almost all the way, then opened the inner door. She put her damp jacket and laptop case inside and turned on the flashlight she carried. Then she shut the inner door almost completely, so that no light escaped from the flashlight being turned on and stepped hunched over back to the outer door. She opened it inward again and made sure that the thick brush growing over the outer door was pulled back together and covered the small door entirely. *There, you'd have to actually push your way in this far to see that there's a door here.* She turned around again and crept back to the inner door, pushed her way in, and closed it tight.

And here I am, "cellaring" once again, she smiled, nostalgically calling up fun and fond memories of years gone by. Of all the places in the entire world, this was actually her most happy place. A childhood retreat from the difficulties and obstacles of the outer world. A magical realm for the imagination. A recreated and private "reality." She could make it that hobbit home. An elf's cottage. A bunny burrow. A badger's bunker. Really, whatever she wanted.

She looked around with tired but delighted eyes at the canned and bottled goods still stored on the shelves, never gotten around to being used, even after all these years. There was a big crock in one corner, sitting on the packed dirt floor, probably still holding pickles in brine. One of the bottom-heavy plank shelves still supported an ancient jug of cider. *Wonder how "hard" that is by now? Those dusty quart jars of peaches and apricots would provide a lot of glazin' for Grandma's coffee cakes, bundt cakes, and fancy breads. Of course, I could glaze now, having learned from her.*

There were a couple of antique, wooden folding chairs in another corner, mostly used by Jane and her, or friends, when they came here "cellaring." She pulled one out toward the center of the cellar and set her weary backside down at last. On another bottom shelf there was a short stack of old burlap bags used for potatoes, carrots, turnips, rutabagas, and carrying items back up to the farmhouse. She pulled them out to make a rough bed with a half-bale of straw left in the cellar. *I don't know how long I'll have to be cellaring until they leave...or find me,* she shuddered. *I might as well try to get some shut-eye.*

Alice probably would have been too frightened and anxious to fall asleep except that she was so completely exhausted, once she stopped, she couldn't keep her eyes open. Toward midnight she drifted off into an uneasy slumber. She had always been a very active dreamer, and perhaps especially with all that had happened earlier that evening, that night was no exception.

It was an unusual dream.

CHAPTER THIRTEEN

Dreams primarily occur in the rapid-eye movement (REM) stage of sleep. Brain activity is high, and physiologically resembles that of being awake. The scientific study of dreaming is called oneirology, and while the actual content and purpose of dreams are not entirely understood, components of the brain activity while sleeping include successions of images, ideas, emotions, sensations, and even attempts at reasoning problems or issues.

It was common for Alice's dreaming to be vivid, in color, and to occur multiple times per night. Mostly they took place in about two hours of REM sleep. That night's phenomenon of dreaming seemed especially vivid, completely out of her control, and disturbing to the point of seeming surreal and threatening.

She dreamed that rough, strong men seized her - perhaps not surprising given the events and dangers of earlier that night - so that she couldn't move her arms and legs. Her head thrashed from side to side, but her body was held almost motionless. But she wasn't outside, not in the yard, the pastureland, nor the woods. She dreamed that she was in some prison-like environment. The men were garbed in dark coveralls, and she couldn't see their masked faces. They were using some substance on her, a truth serum, a psychoactive drug, something to force her to bend to their will. A voice spoke in her ear, and another voice in her other ear. They wanted something from her, to surrender to them. She feared that they were going to kill her once they got what they wanted from her. It was terrifying.

Alice woke up when she felt drops hitting her face from above. But it wasn't a substance being forced upon her, nor any serum or drug. That horrific dream had already melted away so that she was losing any memory of it, leaving behind only an upset feeling as the dream-mist lifted. The drops were coming from the ventilation shaft in the ceiling of the root cellar.

An additional feature of the old root cellar was this ventilation shaft. Without it, the cellar air would have been trapped, stale, and encouraging the growth of molds and mildew. There would have been no air circulation. In the pioneer times in which the cellar had been built, no stout metal pipes or tubes had been available, so the ventilation shaft from cellar up to the top of the natural knoll had been made with a section of hollow log. The base of the piece of log was fastened by stout pegs driven into holes in the ceiling beams. The top, outside end of the log stuck several inches above the ground at the top of the knoll.

But the top end of the hollow log, several inches in diameter, was rough and jagged, so that from the outside it looked up close just like a broken off stump of a small tree. In addition, it, too, was surrounded by the same sort of dense brush that had grown up when no one was there to bother with clearing it. Unless someone bent or lay down and peered down into the top of the log section, it would have been impossible to guess that it led down into some hidden chamber. But it provided enough air intake and exhaust for Alice to be able to breathe comfortably. It also allowed faint light to enter the root cellar when the sun was up, and daylight came upon the knoll. The natural light was very dim in the cellar, but it enabled her to see slightly without having to burn out the batteries of the flashlight too quickly.

Again, in her childhood years that faint light from above seemed to make cellaring somehow more magical, with the dimness and shadows contributing to the images in her imagination. The dark shape in the back corner could become a grumpy old troll, or the fairy godmother resting until summoned by a playful girl. Or for those days when she felt bravely that she could fight and win against gremlins or mischievous elves, the shadows behind the old oats barrel could become those trouble-making spirits.

As her mind cleared wakefully and the disturbing dream faded away almost completely, her initial anxiety lifted with the sun rising outside, and Alice munched on some of the stored foodstuffs that were still edible after opening old jars and boxes. She would have loved her morning coffee, but that would have to wait. She began to think again about her situation, and to wonder what was going on with the hit squad out there on the farm. It was too much to hope that they had just given up and gone away, but in a roughly half-day's time they hadn't caught up to her yet. She gave her laptop case a little pat for reassurance that it and she were still free...and possessing truth and power.

CHAPTER FOURTEEN

The hit squad had searched through the night with their night vision goggles and binoculars. They had worked foot by foot all around the shore of the prairie pothole pond. No tracks or any signs left by the woman or any other human being. Only a few deer tracks, the trail left by a coyote coming down to the water for a drink, duck tracks in the water's edge, and animal droppings.

Alice had guessed and acted correctly. One of the squad had worked through the strip between the root cellar knoll and the marshy shore, but could spot no human footprints or obvious marks of anyone having been in that area. And the old, squat outer door of the root cellar was completely shielded by those thick dwarf willows and brush.

They had gone back and done another sweep in the dark in the yard and around all sides of the farmhouse, but the only trail that could be found was the one she had left from the dangling rope down to the east end of the pond and into the water. They made triply sure that there was no sign leading down the drive and lane to the township road.

They had followed the deep recon protocol of grabbing only fifteen-minute power naps with slugs of espresso-fueled coffee to overcome fatigue and drowsiness. The squad leader called the other two to him in the pasture shortly before dawn.

"Nothing?" he said to confirm with Number Two and Number Three.

"Nope." Number Two replied, and Number Three shook his head negatively.

"Well, at this point only one possibility seems to suggest itself," the leader concluded. "She went into the water and never came out - whether by accidental drowning, or by suicide out of despair. Either way, we don't care, but we need a body to confirm. And we especially need the package. The latter is of supreme importance. She had to have taken it with her into the water."

"So," Number Two said, "this mission needs to shift to search and retrieve. And we need divers and underwater scanning equipment. Do we have those backup plans and preps?"

The squad leader shook his head. "Not at hand. The execution of the assignment was never thought to develop to that extent. But unless she walks up to us and turns herself over with the laptop in the next couple of hours, at 900 this morning the commander himself will board a plane, come here, and bring with him the power to draw upon whatever additional resources might be needed. The highest levels behind this mission aren't about to write this off and just move on without resolution."

"But what about us?" Number Three asked a little apprehensively.

"We might well be out of it and reassigned," the leader shrugged. "And I hope you don't mind a posting somewhere very, very cold and desolate."

And just as he had said, at 900 hours the special ops/black ops commander boarded a commercial airliner at Ronald Reagan Washington National Airport and flew direct to Dane County Regional Airport northeast of Madison, Wisconsin. He then took an SUV rental down U.S. Highway 152 toward the Iowa border. Before long he negotiated county and township roads and in less than two hours, he met up with the hit squad outside the old farmhouse and homestead farm. He immediately took over field command of the mission.

CHAPTER FIFTEEN

That morning as the dim light allowed by the vent log had ever so slightly grown, Alice stretched, worked her aching arms and legs, arched her back and neck, and even moved about in small circles around the cellar and its two center support beams. The size of the interior was only a few yards in diameter, and the height of the place was barely enough to accommodate her five-foot, three-inch height. In fact, at the shelves around the walls she had to duck a little, since the ceiling sloped down slightly from center to walls, which further helped to prevent sagging of the ceiling.

But in addition to wanting to prevent cramping and stiffening, she always seemed to think a bit better when moving, pacing, even jogging...not that she could in such a small space. She again mulled over the certainty that she could not remain cellaring indefinitely. Not only did she lack fresh water and other essentials - *Good Lord, I would almost kill for a bathroom* - but she was sure that somehow they would find her eventually and "terminate the target."

But how can I escape again, successfully avoid them, and get to safety and protection? And most important, how can I get my vital information and evidence to John and out into the world for all to see? How can I possibly know where the bad guys are and what they're doing?

She stopped moving about and stretching and sat down on her folding chair and thought some more. *One thing I know, just like last night, if I'm going to make a move out of here, it has to be in the dark. Whatever night vision or imaging capability they have, the dark of night is at least somewhat better for my prospects than in broad daylight. And I don't think whatever small chance I have will improve if I wait any longer than tonight.*

She finally decided that however slim her chances were, she somehow had to get around them, out to the township road, and head west. *I need to get to the Anderson's, or at least out of range of the bastards' jammer so that I can make a call...*She pulled her cell phone out of her pocket and checked. *Or not, no charger, no power for my phone. Well, Anderson's...or a passing car, truck, bus, anything, so long as it's not the bad guys.*

She decided to open the inner door, in hopes that she could hear some slight noise if any of them came near the outer door. *Although I don't really know what good that would do, to hear them out there. There's only one way in and out of this cellar, so if one of those killers, or all of them, would be right outside, it's not like by hearing them there I could go anywhere. Rush out and announce, "Okay, here I am. You got me?"* But she did it anyway. She just felt better if there was a chance she could hear something.

There was also the matter that she needed to do *something,* even if there wasn't any particular sense or use for it. Most human beings feel a need to *do something* in extreme situations. It's hard to accept that nothing at all can be done. Besides, thinking and doing, even meaningless little actions, seemed to help her avoid being overwhelmed by shock and grief at Victor's fate. If against all odds she actually did escape, there would be time for that later.

She hoped.

CHAPTER SIXTEEN

It was just about noon when the commander huddled with his dejected squad outside the farmhouse. He listened with ill-disguised dissatisfaction to the status report being given by the squad leader, detailing all of the happenings of the botched hit the evening before, the night-long, failed search for the primary target and the all-important package, where they had looked, the methods they had employed, all the pertinent facts of the mission not accomplished, however unpleasant or painful to share.

The commander did not interrupt the squad leader's report, nodded or shook his head at different points, but stayed mostly silent until the leader had concluded. Then he had questions.

"So, no tracks or sign besides those leading into the water?" he confirmed what he had heard.

"No sir, none whatsoever. We searched and re-searched. None. Absolutely..."

The commander held up his hand to stop. No need for

nervous repetition.

"Now I know you employed the goggles and binoculars. What about the thermal imaging, high intensity camera?"

"Well, yes, that is," the squad leader almost sputtered, "we employed that in order to find the hidden safe room in the master bedroom, but, well, it's awfully heavy and bulky to tote around the fields and pond. So, well, not outside."

The commander nodded but didn't add comment. He went on. "Well, you're possibly right. She could have entered the water and whether by accident or suicide, not come out again. I'll have divers and underwater scanning here this afternoon. But you might have thought about mounting that thermal imaging camera on the SUV you've left parked on this drive, for no purpose except to act like a hearse. You could have driven around the place - it has four-wheel drive capability, you know - and scanned for a well-disguised hiding place among these hills. Or at least the trace of a body heat signature where she had passed...not that there would be any by now.

"In fact, you might just do that right now, while we're waiting for the divers, their equipment, and other searchers to show up this afternoon. Start with the farm fields, the hill where she went down to the pond, and work your way around counterclockwise. Go slow. Be thorough. Who knows, you might just find something you missed last night. If nothing else, it'll give you something to do while we're waiting."

The tone of his last comment was not pleasant. *Yup, someplace always cold and desolate,* the squad leader thought to himself as he briskly replied, "Sir, Yes sir!"

The other two members of the squad stayed absolutely quiet and motionless during the entire briefing and questioning, remained that way, and wished to be invisible as they accompanied their leader on the appointed task, but

their thoughts were identical.
   Yup cold, and desolate. Fubar.

CHAPTER SEVENTEEN

The hit squad rigged up the thermal imaging camera with a temporary mount on the tailgate of their SUV. They had put Vic's corpse in a zippered body bag and simply shoved it farther into the back luggage compartment. As ordered, they began at the point where Alice's tracks had entered the marshy strip by the pond the night before. They searched thoroughly, yard by yard, to the east, then curving north, following the ragged contour of the pothole's roughly oblong shape. They checked out hillocks and swales, clumps of dwarf willows and redbrush, brush piles and crisscrossed logs, every place where there could possibly be a hiding spot.

It took a while for the nearest aquatic search and rescue/retrieval team to arrive with their boat trailer, rescue boat, scanning and other equipment, and they weren't ready to begin searching the deeper sections of the nearly forty-acre pond until almost evening. They were also equipped with bright, battery-powered lights mounted on both their boat and tripods, however, so as twilight came upon the scene, they were still able to work. Also, by that time the thermal camera and black op squad had made it a little over half-way around the pothole, proceeding mostly in a westward direction.

In addition, a second three-man squad under the commander's authority had just arrived, bringing with them a third SUV towing a flatbed trailer with an ATV strapped on it.

She has to be somewhere, the commander repeated yet again to himself. *And the package has to be with her. We damn well better find both this evening, or my ass is going to be handed to me as well.*

He went to the back of the third SUV, where the second squad had dutifully brought takeout sandwiches, chips, slaw, potato salad, protein bars and carafes of hot coffee.

He briefed the second squad leader on all that had happened, the status of the search, and strongly emphasized the absolute need to eliminate the principal target and procure the package, no questions, no hesitation, strictly need to know, and he didn't need to know any more than he had just been told.

"Sir, yes sir," was the response expected and dutifully given.

Shortly after dark had settled in for the night, just as the first squad and their SUV and camera had rounded the west corner end of the pothole, the radio squawked alive in his belt holder. "Command, do you copy?"

He responded quickly, "Go ahead, squad one leader, over."

"We may have something. Thermal camera shows a disguised opening, something like a tunnel, and a faint body heat image inside a compartment. Over."

"Copy, squad one leader. Hold your 1020. I'll have light trained on your scene, and squad two and I will be there on the double. Over and out."

He called out to the search and retrieve boat and crew and had them move down to that end of the pond and train their powerful lights in the direction of squad one and the side of the hillock were they had detected their possible target. The commander then gathered the members of squad two. The four of them piled into the ATV and motored along the strip between the marshy wetland and the gently sloping ground along it. At points the strip narrowed so that they splashed in moist, mucky ground with short bull rushes, but the ATV was equipped with deep-lugged tires for conditions just like that. As they rushed to the scene, he indulged in some rare optimism.

It's about time. We better have her now. I damn well need to be able to make a "mission accomplished" report before this night is over.

There was good reason for him to feel some confidence. The camera was highly effective. If it said a body was in the underground compartment, then there surely was.

CHAPTER EIGHTEEN

Everything was appropriately set up when the commander and squad two arrived at the scene on the ATV. Squad one had positioned with their squad leader and number two on either side of the brush in front of the detected entrance. Number three took up a post up on top of the hillock, in a space in the brush up there. Commander radioed again to the search and retrieve boat and had their bright lights shifted a little more exactly at the target area. To be prepared perhaps to excess, he had squad leader two join him directly in front of the entrance area and sent the other two members of squad two to either sloping side of the mound. If any shots were needed, they all knew to be careful of background. There would be no "friendly fire" incidents.

Everything in readiness, he simply said "Proceed" to squad leader two. Second squad leader had taken an axe from the ATV, and he started to chop and clear the tangled brush away from the detected entrance and "tunnel." Before long he had cleared enough to permit access easily. All rifles and sidearms were at the ready. And sure enough, movement in the compartment was detected.

The commander barked loud enough for everyone to hear, "Come out now, hands on your head!"

Rustling was heard, and a squad two member on the north slope of the hillock saw brush begin to move in front of him. "Coming this way," he hollered. And a large, wild badger emerged from a second entrance to her burrow, quickly accompanied by her two almost full-sized juveniles following directly behind her. The three badgers scurried off at the sight of the black-clad operative and fast disappeared in more brush.

"It was badgers," the man reported with another holler, then repeated into his radio mic.

"Goddamn it all to goddamned hell," the commander yelled. "I can't 'f...king' believe this!" The discreetly silent thoughts of the half-dozen operatives on the scene were almost unanimous.

Yup, fubar big time.

CHAPTER NINETEEN

With darkness blackening the inside of the root cellar, Alice was working up her courage to make her move, however risky to the extreme. She readied herself, put on her jacket, made sure that her flashlight was in a pocket, and her lifeless cell phone in the other pocket. Thumb drive number one was still in the hidden compartment in the heel of her running shoe. She once again fastened her laptop by its chain to the bracelet around her wrist, thus making sure that she couldn't drop it to the ground accidentally, nor have it grabbed out of her hand.

In at least some ways she had rather liked cellaring again after all those years, and her nostalgic memories about things like "glazin'" and Grandma teaching her to bake. But she had to believe that her time was almost gone to be safe in there. She had left the inner door open still, again to try to hear outside. And since she hadn't heard anything from the bad guys, it actually startled her when she heard the ATV roar past a few yards away just then.

She stopped short and felt almost paralyzed for a couple of minutes. She was ready to try to make her escape, but what did the machinery noise mean? The roar grew less as she continued to listen. *But does that mean it's gone away, or will it be back soon, or what's going on out there?* But when the fading noise stopped, she had to assume that whatever it was had gone past her and that she was still undetected. After a couple of minutes or so more, she worked up courage to open the outer door slightly and at least to peek out.

And when she did, she could see that the brush and leaves that she had bunched in front of the outer door were still undisturbed. All was dark outside, but a bright glow filtered through the underbrush from down the shore to her left. She hesitantly took a step, being careful not to rustle the bushes so as to create either noise or visible movement. Then another careful step. As quietly as the proverbial mouse, she eased her way until she could get a better look in the direction of that bright glow. She was still mindful to try to keep her silhouette obscured as best she could.

They seem to be concentrated down past the west end of the pond. That must be where that machine or vehicle was headed. And they have that area all lit up. She had no idea what they were up to down there, nor did it really occur to her that the strong lighting made it even more difficult to see anything in her direction in the dark of night.

Alice fervently, desperately, hoped that no remnant guard or sentinel had been left up in the direction of the farmhouse. And there should have been, according to thorough protocol, but the news of a positive imaging detection after so many fruitless hours of searching had perhaps rashly caused the commander and his squads to go all in on the badger burrow being the woman's hiding place. She continued to move as quietly and cautiously as she possibly could upslope in the direction of the house, and it was all she could do to restrain herself from breaking out in a desperate run for her life.

As she finally reached the edge of the yard, she shifted over to the edge of the woods by the house, slipping as silently as she could into the tree line to better hide her form from anyone's view. She really hated to do it, but she forced herself to stop and watch for any movement, and listen for any sound, near the house or drive. Nothing.

Maybe they really didn't leave anyone back to keep watch or guard all their vehicles and equipment. She didn't waste any time or mental energy contemplating that, but continued to move south, keeping to the trees as long as she could. Her route paralleled the drive, and gradually she drew closer to the township road.

Finally, she got to the point where she was forced to leave the woods, cross an open, grassy strip of several yards, and negotiate the roadside ditch with its own rushes, cattails, shallow water and muck. She decided not to chance making any splashing noise or movement of the rushes and cattails trying to push through them. Instead, she took the risk of keeping close to them and creeping over to the culvert over which the farmhouse drive passed.

At last! She thought with a mixture of anxious relief and some partial triumph. And as a tremendous bonus, she saw headlights coming along the township road from the direction of the small town to the west and south. The vehicle seemed to her to take forever to round the bend in the road down past the abandoned, ruined house to the west, and it was several hundred yards away, but getting closer and brighter.

Alice got ready to step out and flag it down. She was actually shaking and virtually jumping up and down, in anticipation of the end of her ordeal. The car or pickup truck passed the abandoned farm and was now only that quarter of a mile away. She stepped out into the pavement and stood in the eastbound lane, waving her right arm frantically while holding on to the laptop with her left hand. Rough, strong hands grabbed her from behind.

CHAPTER TWENTY
University of Iowa Hospital & Psychiatric Clinic
The following Monday...

A man wearing a white lab coat emerged through the "Staff Only" door from the secure, 22-bed inpatient unit of the Psychiatry Department into the family waiting room. He was looking down at a folder on a clipboard, but when he stepped forward into the waiting room he looked up at one of the two men sitting nervously in the chairs around the walls, then at the other, and asked, "Mr., ah, Chernowsky?"

The early middle-aged man on the left side of the room replied, "Here." The older man on the right side looked disappointed and bent his head back down rather dejectedly.

The psychiatrist invited Victor Chernowsky to follow him back to a small conference room behind a locked door with a heavy glass window.

"Please sit down," the M.D. gestured toward one of the eight chairs at the center table. The psychiatrist sat opposite Vic and looked down again at the patient folder he had placed on the table in front of him. "I'm Doctor Jenkins. And you're here in regard to, ah, Alice Louis. Alice is your...?"

"My wife, yes. We've been married almost nine years now."

"And you understand that Alice is hospitalized and confined here because she was brought in last night out of concern for her immediate well-being, as well as the safety of others, because of what appears to be a psychotic episode?"

"Yes," Vic affirmed a bit nervously, "She has a mental health history of acute paranoid schizophrenia ever since young adulthood..." He would have gone on, but the doctor gently interrupted him, obviously having his own agenda to pursue.

"I can see that, although I'm still in the process of familiarizing myself with her history and chart information. Before I go on, however, I might just mention that 'paranoid schizophrenia' is a sub-type categorization that hasn't really been used in the United States since, oh, about 2013. We refer to this chronic mental disorder now simply as 'schizophrenia.' As I would suppose you already know, schizophrenics withdraw from reality. But yes, persecutory delusions are very often manifested in her mind and emotions. And those delusions are usually accompanied by hallucinations and perceptual disturbances..."

Vic wanted both to be respectful and to find out all that he could about his wife's current condition or status, but he couldn't help but feel a bit impatient with what felt like it was a Schizophrenia 101 lecture to an ignorant spouse. He had been dealing with his wife's mental health challenges for years now, as lovingly and supportively as he possibly could. It was his turn to gently interrupt.

"Yes, she has that typical experience of delusions, hallucinations, hearing voices in her head that aren't really there...at least not coming from outside her. And at times she has suffered in terms of her ability to function in her teaching at the University and other aspects of daily life, but treatment has usually improved her quality of life and work..."

The doctor of psychiatry interrupted again. "And I want to learn about that treatment history, as well as what took place in the incident that brought her in here last night.

"Now she's been prescribed neuroleptics among her medications, I assume?"

"Yes," Vic affirmed. "For, oh, probably five years or more at this point. And it's generally managed her delusions, hallucinations and paranoia fairly well. At least relieved both frequency and intensity."

"Okay, good. Well we may have to adjust the prescription dosage. And has she been sticking strictly to the prescription protocol, instructions? As I'm sure you know, it's not uncommon for patients with mental health disorders to lapse or self-adjust when they are feeling better or haven't been afflicted for a time.

"And one of the common reasons for not being sufficiently disciplined about meds is that long-term use of antipsychotics can present adverse effects like involuntary movement disorders, or often of concern to women especially, weight gain."

"No, she understands the importance of maintaining careful treatment, and not to vary from prescriptions or instructions unless conferring with her physician first." But then Vic hesitated and looked away, then back at the M.D. "Although she was feeling so 'up' near the end of last week about our plans to spend the weekend at her old, family homestead and farm out on the prairie. I have to wonder now if she might have relaxed her usual discipline, maybe subconsciously - sorry, I guess I'm lapsing into your specialty..."

"No, that's okay," the psychiatrist said, "Go on."

"Well, maybe subconsciously in a way she wasn't feeling the need to be so careful with her meds. You know, feeling so good and almost 'high' about our little getaway."

"That sounds like the sort of behavior exhibited by my patients with bipolar disorder, but the lines between these disorders are not always strictly drawn. Now I'd also like to get a more complete picture of her recent history and activity…"

But another interruption occurred at that point. A psychiatric nurse opened the door.

"I'm sorry to interrupt, doctor, but may I confer with you for a moment?"

Dr. Jenkins looked at Vic, "Please excuse me. Stay right here, and I'll be back momentarily." He picked up Alice's patient folder and left the conference room, following the nurse.

The "moment" stretched into more like ten-fifteen minutes, but he finally returned as Vic was forced to wonder what was going on that had disturbed his consult.

"Sorry about that," the psychiatrist said as he retook his place at the table. He opened up the folder again and Vic couldn't help but notice that there were fresh notes added while the doctor was absent. Vic immediately thought, *Was that about Alice?*

And it was.

CHAPTER TWENTY-ONE

V ic felt as though the psychiatrist's next words had a slightly more alarming tone to them.

"I was called away," he explained, "because your wife has become catatonic. She experienced something like a seizure, exhibited abnormal movement, 'twitching,' certainly arising from her still disturbed mental state of schizophrenia. She was making repetitive actions, but in a state of immobility. Catatonia is not usually prominent with her schizophrenia but can definitely manifest related to violent imagery. We've treated her with a sedative called 'benzodiazephine,' which is also used to ease anxiety."

Vic was much more alarmed at that explanation. "Ah, what brought this on? How long will it last? Can I see her? Is it apt to happen again?..."

Dr. Jenkins tried to slow down his torrent of questions. "As I said, it's probably related to whatever violent imagery she was experiencing in her hallucinations. It may last for some hours, but in the meantime, we are restraining her for her own safety and that of others. It's probably best that you not see her quite yet, until she's calmed and can accept stimuli and respond. But yes, it can happen again. It's vitally important that she be stabilized with treatment."

"May I ask what, if anything, she said or was doing as this happened?"

"The nurses and orderlies who responded to this episode reported that she only said two words before becoming uncommunicative: 'cellaring' and 'glazing.' And then it seemed as though her eyes glazed over in her catatonic state. Do those words carry any meaning for you?"

"Actually, they do," Vic said. "She loved the old pioneer root cellar on the family homestead out on the prairie as a young girl, visiting her grandparents. She used to go there and play with her sister and friends, and regarded it as a magical place. Her 'happy place' she used to call it. They called the experience 'cellaring.'

"And as far as the word 'glazin,' her grandmother taught her how to bake - marvelous, delicious fruit cakes, coffee cakes, buns and rolls, fancy breads - and Grandma would have Alice bring up jars of canned fruits like peaches, apricots, plums from the root cellar to make glaze toppings for those goodies. But was there anything else?"

"Well, one rather strange happening the nurse reported. It seems that just before the catatonia seized her, maybe as it was beginning, your wife had been left alone in her room. Now let me hasten to add that she had been quiet and not agitated, not restrained at that point. But she got up, slipped unnoticed out of her room and over to the nurses' station. No one was at the station at that time, so Alice was unobserved. For some reason, undoubtedly related to her delusional state, she snatched one of the station's laptop computers, closed it and carried it back to her room.

"Now no damage occurred, nothing disturbed on the

computer, and what she had done was quickly detected. But when one of the nurses and an orderly proceeded to retrieve it out of her tenacious grip, she fought to keep it and repeated, 'my notes, my notes.' She resisted giving it up with all of her strength, and it was at that point that the catatonia really set in, and those words, 'cellaring' and 'glazing.'

"Well, this has been quite a bit for now. Do you want to continue to wait here until you can see her, Mr. Cher..." The physician glanced back at his papers, "Chernowsky, right?"

"Right. Well, Dr. Chernowsky, actually, but I'm not usually that formal."

"Physician?" Dr. Jenkins raised an eyebrow slightly as if surprised.

"No, modern literature at the university," Vic said.

He wasn't sure the psychiatrist thought that counted, as he immediately turned back to his papers. Vic still had a question.

"So back to treatment if we may. You mentioned at the outset adjusting her medications. Is there other treatment you envision?"

"We're trying to evaluate the type of catatonia she's manifesting. The most common is akinetic, which would be consistent with staring blankly, eyes glazing over, lack of response, but she had obviously demonstrated another type called 'excited' catatonia, having displayed pointless, repetitive movements, agitation, and being combative. Excited catatonics may also be delirious, but since her schizophrenia is experienced with hallucinations and delusions, it can be challenging to differentiate what's caused by her schizophrenia and what is a result of a type of catatonia. The two may coincide. We'll sort that out and treat as best we can determine.

"I should tell you, however, Mr. Chernowsky, that if the sedatives don't work to help bring Alice out of this catatonic episode, and the catatonia seems to be severe and multi-type, it may become necessary to put her to 'sleep' and use electroconvulsive therapy, which we often refer to simply as ECT."

Vic winced perceptively. "I remember an older relative who was subjected to what back then they referred to as 'electro-shock,' and it wasn't the most pleasant or effective procedure."

"Rest assured," the psychiatrist said, "techniques have advanced and been refined considerably over the years. Basically, if that treatment seems necessary, we place electrodes on her head and send carefully controlled and measured electrical impulses to the brain. The goal, of course, is to adjust the natural electrical circuits and impulses of the neurological system."

"Now this is obviously not my field of specialty," Vic stated the obvious, "but in the years following my relative's experience with electro-shock therapy, I tried to read up to some extent on the effectiveness of ECT, and is it true that it has not been extensively studied in its effect on schizophrenia? Also, that it actually causes something of a seizure of the brain?"

Dr. Jenkins seemed to stiffen ever-so-slightly as if he was being challenged by a layman regarding his field of expertise. "I assure you, again, that you can leave that up to us." He apparently decided that more than enough time had been spent in this consultation. He got up, closing his file and folder.

"Follow-up would also include psychotherapy with me, once Alice has stabilized enough to be discharged and go home. Appointments would be here in our clinic, beginning with one-on-one sessions between her and me, but later including you, possibly other close family members. Now if you'll excuse me, I have other patients I have to deal with."

All-in-all, Vic felt as though the consultation had been informative, and it seemed as though Alice would receive thorough evaluation, diagnosis, treatment, and overall care, but despite being better informed and knowledgeable than probably the average family member of a schizophrenic person, the entire experience was extremely upsetting, worrisome, and frustrating. Dealing with mental health disorders was very difficult for both patient and loved ones, and not to be unfair in the least, he had to wonder just how well the mental health professionals were able to treat and improve persons' mental health and well-being in their lives.

He decided he needed a break, made sure that the nurse and receptionist had his cell number and understood his desire to see Alice as soon as they could make it possible, and left to get a bite to eat. He also felt the need to think seriously about what positive steps he could take for her now and in the future. He was prepared to provide all of the love, support, and helpful efforts he could possibly could in her behalf. Nothing was more important to him than Alice.

CHAPTER TWENTY-TWO

Ten weeks after Alice was released from
the psychiatric hospital and returned home to Coralville...

The sedatives eased Alice Louis's catatonia, although it was impossible to tell whether it was the treatment that helped her come out of the condition, or whether her brain's own chemistry, circuitry, and natural healing power was the truly decisive force. In any case, while her schizophrenia would require constant care and treatment for the rest of her life, the ECT therapy was not used.

Along with her adjusted medications, follow-up appointments at the clinic, weeks of psychotherapy counseling sessions, and a lot more reading and research to better understand her mental health disorder and how to best live and work with it, Vic and she discussed what they could do to make her life in general as supportive and therapeutic as possible.

One loss that concerned Alice was the disappearance of her personal, encrypted laptop. Somehow it had gone missing the weekend that Vic and she were planning to make their trip into the country. Memory of what she did with it, where she last saw it, or what might have happened to it seemed completely lost in the turmoil of her psychotic episode. Of less concern but still bothersome was the misplacing at the hospital of the plastic pull-tie bag that contained her clothes, belt, jacket, and shoes at the time of her admission. The psychiatric unit staff was apologetic, and she was promised by a representative of the hospital that they would reimburse her for replacement items of similar value.

But the biggest loss confronted them once home. It was a hard decision, but since the old prairie homestead, the farmhouse with its unusual safe room, and the old root cellar had all seemed to have a part in her psychotic episode - even if only in her mind - they agreed after weeks of wrestling with it, pros and cons, back and forth, that they would put the historic place up for sale. It only took three months until the second prospective buyers who toured the house and acreage fell instantly in love with the prospects of having a place in the country that would give them both an escape from the busyness of Madison, Wisconsin, and a future retirement location and hobby farm.

When the impending sale was firmly in escrow, Vic and Alice made a final day trip to the homestead to say "goodbye." Among other things, the final visit was therapeutic in the sense that it reinforced the reality that her terrifying hallucination and lingering trauma was no longer something to haunt her with false memories. She even checked out the old root cellar and indulged in a little well-seasoned nostalgia about her old "cellaring" days.

It was also genuinely sad, however, because they had learned that the new owners were planning eventually to have her grandfather's grand old house torn down. They liked the "quaint" feel of it, but having the money to do so, they wanted to build a state-of-the-art modern home with unique country architecture, all solar power, completely energy efficient, sweeping curved triple-paned windows and wide patio doors, something worthy of *Architectural Digest*. They also didn't see the sense of the homemade safe room. They weren't concerned about the threat of fierce thunderstorms or tornados.

About two months after Alice and Vic made their goodbye visit to the place, the professional demolition crew and heavy machinery started in on the stately house. With large, powerful bulldozer and heavy crane they punched in outer walls and studding. It didn't take long before the safe room came crashing down on the pile of rubble, still remarkably intact due to its very sturdy beams, floor and ceiling extra-heavy framing, and interior supports.

Also crashing down, of course, was the sharply pitched attic and roof. And of no particular notice to the demolition crew came the antique, brass rooster weathervane in the center of the roof. It disappeared unseen into the pile of rubble and debris. But if anyone had scrutinized its inglorious fall - no longer proclaiming the shifting directions of winds and coming storms - there was no way they would have seen a small, mostly black object ejected from under the base anchoring the classic weathervane to the roof ridge.

It was a SanDisk Ultra USB 3.0 thumb drive, sixty-four gigabytes. It disappeared as a tiny part of all the dust and trash that was soon scooped up by a large, toothed bucket on the end of the crane and dumped into a giant, multi-wheeled dump truck bound for a construction debris land fill. Only angels in heaven would ever know what data was stored on it.

The End

EPILOGUE

The novella you have just read deserves at least two follow up points, I believe.

First is that mental health is one of the largest, most critical issues among human beings worldwide. Although it's impossible to have exact figures, it is estimated by mental health agencies around the globe that close to a billion people - roughly twelve to thirteen percent of the world population of 7.8 billion human beings (as of March, 2020) - suffer some mental or substance abuse disorder. In terms of specific disorder type, the largest number of people have anxiety disorder, estimated at about four percent of global population.

Schizophrenia and psychotic disorders alone are estimated to afflict at least one percent of the Earth's people, with 20 million people affected by schizophrenia. It is safe to say that the great majority of what is truly an overlooked pandemic goes untreated.

In the United States of America alone, it's estimated that approximately one and a quarter percent of the population, or three and a third million, have schizophrenia disorder. And almost half of American adults will experience some mental illness during their lifetime. As of 2019 that amounted to about 44 million people in any one year.

Whether globally or nationally, the numbers and percentages are mind-numbing, enough to cause a person's eyes to glaze over and encourage whatever form of "cellaring" one prefers. Perhaps even worse, only about forty percent of Americans who had a mental disorder in any recent year received any professional health care or other helpful services.

It's commonly known among most people that mental illness, mental disorders, even relatively temporary mental difficulty and distress, are extremely unacceptable in many families, groups of people, and society at large. This tremendously common, limiting, and often debilitating phenomenon is "hidden" or "covered up" by victims, families, coworkers, even friends whether close or casual. A person usually has no problem admitting to having a cold, sniffle, or having to take a sick day. Very few feel comfortable disclosing that they are dealing with a mental disorder or illness. The sense of shame is powerful as to be avoided at all cost for many. And yet, the statistics can't be denied. Most people in America - and worldwide, for that matter - either suffer from mental health challenges and illness themselves or have someone in their close family who does. It probably expands to 100% when the circle is extended to encompass friends, acquaintances, and associates.

And while the phenomenon of crushing shame has lessened at least to some degree in American society, the respected publication *Psychology Today (2018)* underlines that it was not so many years ago that family members who were afflicted by psychological problems were almost universally considered a shame to the family and were often hidden away in insane asylums, mental hospitals and wards, secure facilities, and certainly in prisons.

In fact, any husband in a highly patriarchal society had the right to sign his wife into a permanent ward without her consent, and even to order ECT. Again, matters have shown some improvement. For instance, the often too-lightly dismissed "shell shock" and "battle fatigue" afflicting military personnel and others has become recognized as PTSD, post-traumatic stress syndrome, and is better diagnosed and treated today. But on the other hand, it is generally recognized that a tremendous number of America's homeless and "street people" are suffering constantly from mental disorders and are often veterans with PTSD. The shame actually needs to be owned by all of us, especially including all levels of government.

Regarding the Second follow up point, it needs to be recognized as irrefutable truth and fact that democracy and, again, all levels of government, power and influence in the United States of America have become enslaved to greed, short-term and long-term profit, and the corrupting effect of money that buys everything. The political struggle in the nation is not so much between conservative and liberal, authoritarian and progressive, capitalism and socialism...as it is between genuine democracy of the people, for the people, and by the people...and out-of-control plutocracy, a society and nation ruled by a few people, corporations, and societies of great wealth and lust for more. Ironically, plutocracy is not necessarily rooted in any established political philosophy, but can be easily reduced to "I have, you don't, and I want as much of what little you have as I can get." Or in the words and daily mantra of the world's richest man of a previous generation, "I'd be really happy with just a little bit more."

Whether addressed as "wealth distribution," fairness of income, compensation more equal and commensurate with need and true worth, fair trade, campaign finance reform, consumer protection, a "new deal," or a great host of other legitimate issues and perspectives, the crisis needs to be brought into the light of day, diagnosed, treated, and cured. There should be no personal, family, society or national shame to Justice and Righteousness.

ABOUT THE AUTHOR

The Rev. Dr. David Quincy Hall is a retired Presbyterian pastor living with his beloved wife, the Rev. Maxine, their daughters, son-in-law, grandson, and two dogs in Oceanside, Southern California.

David is a lifelong civil rights activist, environmentalist, and social justice advocate. His first two experiences in pastoral ministry were in the inner-city areas of San Francisco, California and Pittsburgh, Pennsylvania in the 1960's. He has dialogued with and lobbied members of Congress in Washington, D.C. and state legislators and committees regarding these issues.

His parish ministry was with congregations across the country in Pennsylvania, Michigan, Iowa, Wisconsin and California, in diverse settings including metropolitan, inner city, suburban, medium-sized and small cities, small town, rural, and the North Woods.

One of many critical issues the Rev. Dr. Hall has addressed in his life and ministry is the pandemic of mental illness and disorders that affects most of the American and world population. Cellaring came out of a burden on his heart and mind for all the persons he's known and ministered to with those afflictions. It is set in the American prairie region in Iowa and Southwestern Wisconsin in which he studied, worked and pastored years ago.

Like his series of murder mystery novels, *Death Most Unholy*, including the paperback books: *Death Comes to the Rector*, *Death Crashes the Wedding*, and *Death Stalks the Forest*, this novella is in that genre, but with a very powerful and pertinent message.